TO **OLIVER**

HAPPY BIRTHDAY

FROM

HAPPY BIRTHDAY

Shake the book really fast....

Come on, Oliver,
let's **POP** the balloons.

Ready?
Set?
Go!

Press here
OLIVER

HA, HA, Oliver, it's upside down!

Turn the book to see who's monkeying around.

Ready for your big present, Oliver?

Tilt the book this way....

To the Birthday GIRL Oliver

Happy Birthday, Oliver!

Now take a big breath in and **BLOW** out your candles.

3, 2, 1...

HAPPY BIRTHDAY

OLIVER

MY FAVORITE PARTY GAME IS:

HAPPY BIRTHDAY

MY AMAZING PARTY GUESTS ARE CALLED:

Draw your cake

HAPPY BIRTHDAY OLIVER!

Illustrated by Hazel Quintanilla
Designed by Nicky Scott

Copyright © Orangutan Books Ltd 2019

Put Me In The Story is a registered trademark of Sourcebooks, Inc.
All rights reserved.

Published by Put Me In The Story, a publication of Sourcebooks, Inc.
P.O. Box 4410, Naperville, Illinois 60567-4410
(630) 536-1104
www.putmeinthestory.com

Date of Production: March 2020
Run Number: 5017370
Printed and bound in China (GD)
10 9 8 7 6 5 4 3 2 1

FSC
www.fsc.org

MIX
Paper from
responsible sources
FSC® C117745

put me
in the story
Bestselling books starring your child!
www.putmeinthestory.com